Lucky G
and the
Melancholy Quokka

How Play Therapy can Help Children with Depression

Written by Amy Wilinski-Lyman
Illustrated by Leela Green

Loving Healing Press

Ann Arbor, MI

Library of Congress Cataloging-in-Publication Data

Names: Lyman, Amy Wilinski, 1973- author. | Green, Leela J.
Title: Lucky G and the melancholy quokka : how play therapy can help
    children with depression / Amy Wilinski Lyman ; [illustrated by] Leela
    J. Green.
Description: Ann Arbor, MI : Loving Healing Press, [2021] | Audience: Ages
    5-8 years. | Audience: Grades 2-3. | Summary: While visiting a friend in
    Australia, Lucky G, a psychotherapist in the form of a raven, meets Blue
    the Quokka and uses play therapy to address the depression that keeps
    Blue from smiling.
Identifiers: LCCN 2020045387 (print) | LCCN 2020045388 (ebook) | ISBN
    9781615995417 (paperback) | ISBN 9781615995424 (hardcover) | ISBN
    9781615995431 (kindle edition) | ISBN 9781615995431 (epub)
Subjects: CYAC: Stories in rhyme. | Depression, Mental--Fiction. | Play
    therapy--Fiction. | Quokka--Fiction.
Classification: LCC PZ8.3.L984 Luc 2021 (print) | LCC PZ8.3.L984 (ebook)
    | DDC [E]--dc23
LC record available at https://lccn.loc.gov/2020045387
LC ebook record available at https://lccn.loc.gov/2020045388

ISBN 978-1-61599-541-7 paperback
ISBN 978-1-61599-542-4 hardcover
ISBN 978-1-61599-543-1 eBook

Published by
Loving Healing Press
5145 Pontiac Trail
Ann Arbor, Mi 48105

info@LHPress.com
www.LHPress.com
toll free (USA/CAN) 888-761-6268
Fax 734-663-6861

Distributed by Ingram (USA/CAN/AU) and Bertram's Books (UK/USA)

Dedication

TO ZACH, DREW AND KENDALL.
I will always love you more.
To anyone who has ever felt really really sad and
didn't know why. Don't give up. It's not all in your head.
Keep fighting. It is so worth it.

There's a cool, fun bird known as Lucky G
He's a smart, caring raven with a Ph.D.
A doctor who uses talking and stuff
To help out young friends when their feelings get rough.

Lucky planned a vacation
To see his good friend Drew
Way down under in Australia
Where Drew lived at a zoo.

Lucky put on his bush hat
For some real Aussie flair
Then flew over the Pacific
'Til he saw kangaroos down there!

Lucky swooped down when he saw his old pal Drew
Who really stands out in a crowd
At six feet (that's two meters) tall, you can see
Emus are quite big and they're loud!

Drew grunted, "G'day to you, mate!"
I'm so glad you're here, Lucky G
It's been far too long, my dear raven friend
And there's someone I think you should see.

"I want you to meet Blue the Quokka,
Quite the happiest creature on earth
You mainly find them here in Australia
Ours was born on an island near Perth."

"I know all about quokkas," said Lucky G
"They are the latest Internet sensation
With grinning teeth from ear-to-ear
They're known in every nation!"

Drew shook his big head slowly
"I'm afraid Blue lives up to his name
So sad every day, with no end in sight
Can you help him get back to his game?"

They hurried to meet the sad quokka
To see what Doc Lucky could do
He flew over the outback exhibit
To see what was troubling Blue.

Left at Kendall the Flamingo, straight by Zach the Dingo
And right past the platypus called Bruce
But where was that quokka? There, hiding
Tucked behind swinging vines that were loose.

"Hello, Blue. I'm Doctor Lucky G
Yes, I'm a raven with a Ph.D.
I help animals when things get tough
By listening to them when life gets rough.

"I'm here to listen kindly
Tell me of your quokka ways
Take your time to share your feelings
Even if it takes days and days."

Blue the Quokka smiled and softly sighed
"I'm not sure where to start
While everyone thinks that I'm happy
I feel like I'm falling apart."

"I used to zip high through the trees
I once loved to climb and have fun
Now there are times when people come by
And I don't want to see anyone."

"People come from far and wide
Yelling 'Smile, you quokka, quokka, quokka'
They take a photo with me, shouting
Smile, you rocka rocka rocka!"

"But even though my face is grinning
They can't see my rocka has gone away
My smile is a lie, 'cause deep down inside
I don't even want to play."

"The zookeepers are trying hard
To help me get back my groove
But it doesn't seem to be working
There are days that I can barely move."

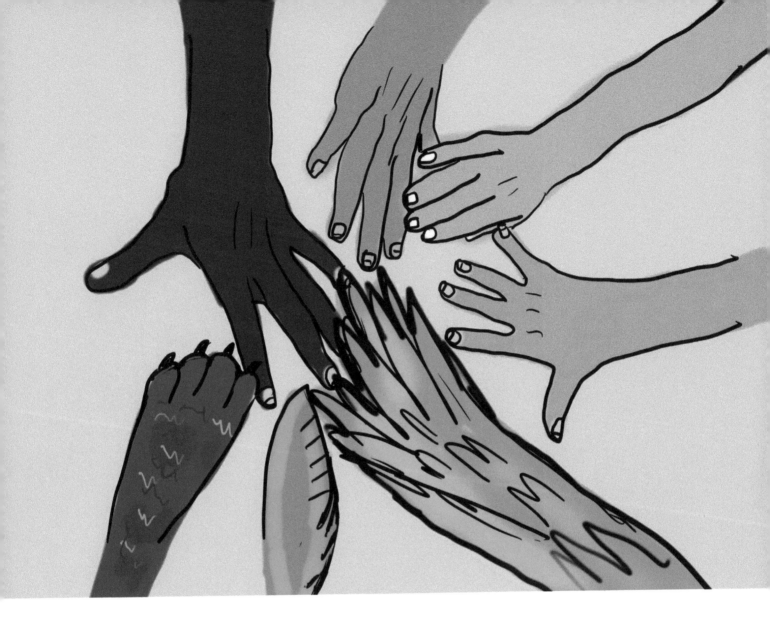

Lucky G said with compassion
"Dear quokka, your feelings have a name
Depression strikes grownups and kids too
Even though it might not look the same."

"With depression, the sads just won't go away
Leaving bed feels an impossible feat
But I have some tools that may help you
And this sadness we can surely beat."

Blue nodded his head, "yes, I'll try it," he said
"Please make my sadness go away
Tell me what I need to do
So I can smile again today."

"Dear Blue, my plan is not a quick fix
Depression can last for a while
However, we'll work close together
To help you get back your true smile."

For days and days, and lots of plays
Cars, games, dolls, and bubbles
Lucky and Blue worked on those skills
To help with the quokka's troubles.

Playing can help a doctor figure out
Some reasons you might be depressed
But Lucky told Blue of what else he could do
To help him get back to his best.

"You should get good sleep, eat well and on time
Drink water and sometimes take medicine
And here's something else that's important
Don't miss out on your therapy sessions."

"With therapy, you can work out problems
Through playing or simply by talking
You might spend some time in an office
Or you might go outside and go walking."

With Lucky's help, Blue figured out
His sadness was not for always
"But Doctor G, when you fly away
Who will help me through the bad days?"

"My family is gone, I have no close pals
A sad quokka doesn't have many friends
Lucky G said, "Let's meet your zoo neighbors
Before my Australian vacation ends."

Blue didn't go far to find a new friend
Next door, to be honest with you
Who knew the koala was also feeling sad?
He was waiting for a friend like Blue.

With a friend to play and share with
And tools to help them muddle through
Blue realized he felt different now
"Hey, I'm smiling INSIDE, too!"

Lucky G got ready to leave the zoo
Knowing Blue's mind was in a better place
He had a good time with his old friend Drew
Who promised to keep him filled in on Blue's case.

If you feel sad and can't set your feelings free
Look around for a friend like the raven Lucky G,
Someone you can turn to when things get tough
Who will listen to you when life gets rough.

Depression can strike anyone
But with help, we can work hard to fight it
Please share your feelings with someone you trust
There's truly no reason to hide it.

Parent and Caregiver Resources
Identifying Symptoms of Depression in Children

Occasionally being sad or feeling hopeless is a part of every child's life. If these feelings are persistent or your child doesn't seem like themselves, it's time to take a closer look. In the United States alone, nearly 2.0 million children between the ages of 3 and 17 have a depression diagnosis.

Behaviors often seen in children with depression include:

- Feeling sad, hopeless, or irritable a lot of the time
- Not wanting to do or enjoy doing fun things
- Showing changes in eating patterns – eating a lot more or a lot less than usual
- Showing changes in sleep patterns – sleeping a lot more or a lot less than normal
- Showing changes in energy – being tired and sluggish or tense and restless a lot of the time
- Having a hard time paying attention
- Feeling worthless, useless, or guilty
- Showing self-injury and self-destructive behavior

Some children may not talk about their helpless and hopeless thoughts and may not appear sad. Depression might also cause a child to make trouble or act unmotivated, causing others not to notice that the child is depressed or to incorrectly label the child as a troublemaker or lazy.

It is important to track these symptoms and not dismiss them as acting out or some kind of ploy. Experts say if symptoms last more than two weeks, seek the help of a professional.

Source: Centers for Disease Control and Prevention (cdc.gov)

Starting a Discussion

Depression can be hard to talk about. But if a child is depressed, having a conversation about getting help can make a big difference. Use these tips to start talking.

Show you care.

- "How are you feeling? I'm here to listen to you and support you."
- Let me tell you all the things I love about you."
- "I'd really like to spend more time with you. Let's take a walk, grab something to eat, or go to a movie."

Offer hope.

- "You're not alone. Many people have depression – it's nothing to be ashamed of."
- "Depression can be treated. Getting help is the best thing you can do."
- "There are different ways to treat depression, including therapy and medicine, painting, even playing!"

Offer to help.

- "Let me help you figure out what's going on. We can start by making an appointment with your doctor."
- "You can call or text me at any time if you need support – or if you just want to talk."
- "It's important for you to get enough sleep, eat well and exercise, I can do this with you. It's important for everybody. You're not alone. We are in this together."

Ask life-saving questions.

- "Have you felt hopeless or thought about hurting yourself recently? I'm here for you." Let's call the National Suicide Prevention Lifeline at 1-800-273-TALK (1-800-273-8255)."

Source: U.S. Dept. of Health and Human Services (health.gov)

Avoiding Isolation

Loneliness is a common experience with 80% of the population under 18 years of age. A lack of interaction and connection can worsen depression symptoms. Some children are shy and find it hard to make the first move with new friends.

To help with this process:

- Inspire your child to join a club at school or attend activities
- Give them ideas on attending various social events
- Encourage play dates and sleepovers at your house
- Organize family gatherings

Whatever makes your child stay in contact with people will help. Just remember, don't leave loneliness unattended. It won't go away on its own.

Source: Centers for Disease Control and Prevention (cdc.gov)

Common Myths

1. Myth: Chronic Sadness Will Go Away on Its Own.

Chronic sadness could mean a child has pediatric depression, which cannot be willed away. Ignoring the problem doesn't help either. Depression is a serious, but treatable, illness that requires professional help.

2. Myth: Talking About Sadness with Children Can Make Things Worse.

Talking about sadness with your child can help reduce symptoms by validating their feelings and experience. It also helps to teach them about their feelings and how to name them. Support and encouragement let children know they're not alone, and that they are loved and cared for.

3. Myth: The Risk of Suicide For Children Is Exaggerated.

Suicide is the 2nd leading cause of death in youth ages 10 to 24. Suicide is significantly linked to depression, so early diagnosis and treatment is a vital aspect of prevention.

4. Myth: There Are No Proven Treatments for Pediatric Depression.

Studies show talk therapy treatments like play therapy, family therapy, and individual therapy offer significant improvements for children who experience depression. Children and families who are involved with psychotherapy learn how to identify sad feelings, express them in healthy ways, and learn interventions to cope better.

5. Myth: Depressed Children Cannot Lead Productive Lives.

Children with depression can grow up to live full, productive lives, especially if they receive the treatment and support they need.

Source: National Alliance on Mental Illness (nami.org)

Resources You Can Call On

National Suicide Prevention Lifeline

Call 1-800-273-8255

Available 24 hours every day

NAMI Helpline

Call 1-800-950-6264

NAMI, the National Alliance on Mental Illness, is the nation's largest grassroots mental health organization dedicated to building better lives for the millions of Americans affected by mental illness. To find a support group near you, log onto nami.org to find your local chapter.

Crisis Text Line

Text CONNECT to 741741.

Crisis text line is free, 24/7 support for those in crisis, connecting people in crisis to trained crisis counselors.

Association for Play Therapy

 The APT directory includes all individuals who have obtained the Registered Play TherapistTM or Registered Play Therapist-SupervisorTM credential through APT who are state licensed clinical mental health practitioners.

Look for a play therapist near you:

https://www.a4pt.org

YouthLine

Text teen2teen to 839863, or call 1-800-852-8336

YouthLine provides a safe space for children and adults ages 11 to 21, to talk through any issues they may be facing, including eating disorders, relationship or family concerns, bullying, sexual identity, depression, self-harm, anxiety and thoughts of suicide.

Crisis Mode

- If your child has a plan to hurt themself or has already self-harmed, you will need to act quickly and kindly.
- Do not leave them alone.
- Call your doctor's office.
- If needed, call 911 for emergency services.
- Go to the nearest emergency room.

About the Author

Amy Wilinski-Lyman lives in Michigan with her three awesome children: Zach, Drew, and Kendall; and her big fluffy orange cat, Marshall. Lucky G and the Melancholy Quokka is her second book. The first, Lucky G and the Sunbeam Girl, was published in 2019. Amy became a mental health warrior in 2016 after she was diagnosed with bipolar disorder. Through her books and online presence (www.facebook.com/luckygbookseries), she wants to show parents and children living with mental illness that there is hope. A good treatment plan can be game changing. A fantastic support system is also extremely helpful. Amy credits her family's love, encouragement, and patience with helping her to reach her goals. Readers can email the author at amylynnlyman@gmail.com.

About the Illustrator

Leela J. Green is an artist and illustrator based in Michigan. She is excited to use her talents and vibrant style to bring the Lucky G books to life and to help young readers and their families deal with mental illness. As someone who also struggles with mental illness, Leela knows the power of art to communicate difficult feelings. She hopes Lucky G can help people find hope and to rise above depression to find joy. Readers can email the illustrator at carson08green@yahoo.com.

CPSIA information can be obtained
at www.ICGtesting.com
Printed in the USA
BVHW090723281020
591953BV00003B/65

9 781615 995417